MY BEST FRIEND

by **P. Mignon Hinds**

illustrated by **Cornelius Van Wright**

*This Little Golden Storybook™ was published
in cooperation with Essence Communications, Inc.*

A GOLDEN BOOK • NEW YORK
Golden Books Publishing Company, Inc., Racine, Wisconsin 53404

Omar isn't my best friend anymore. Today he made me really mad. He broke my favorite model airplane—and he didn't even say, "I'm sorry."

And yesterday we had a race. Even though I thought I was first, he kept saying *he* was first.

At my party he took the biggest piece of cake!

And he always grabs the window seat!

And when that *new* boy came to our class,
Omar kept talking to him. He even played
with him at recess. That made me mad, too.

Maybe I won't ever speak to Omar again.

But . . . when I was the new kid in class and my pencil broke, Omar gave me his. That's how we became friends.

When I got sick, Omar gave me his favorite baseball card.

Omar also tells the funniest jokes.
Sometimes I laugh so hard, I can't stop.
And Omar always laughs at my jokes, too.

Whenever I stay over at Omar's house,
he lets me play with all his toys.

And when Omar's Mom makes peanut butter cookies, he always shares them with me. He knows how much I like them.

We-l-l-l . . . I guess Omar *is* still my best friend. Sometimes we don't get along, but most times we do. I'm going to call him now— maybe he wants to ride bikes!